Pop Star Heather Fideler has had enough. After a painful divorce, she decides to spend Christmas, once her best time of year, on a remote island with no Wi-Fi or tabloids where no one knows who she is. The plan is to keep her head down and let the holidays slide by, but not if the locals have anything to say about it.

Heather's Haven
Copyright © 2023 T.S. McNeil
ISBN: 978-1-4874-4091-6
Cover art by Martine Jardin

Published by eXtasy Books Inc

Look for us online at:
www.eXtasybooks.com

HEATHER'S HAVEN

BY

T.S. MCNEIL

DEDICATION

For Helen McNeil and Richard Curtis for all the support and inspiration.

CHAPTER ONE: LIKE A BROKEN PENCIL

Holidays were never a big deal in Heather Fideler's world. Reared by two of the strictest Calvinists in Christendom, she'd long held the opinion that vacations were for people who didn't like their jobs.

Festivals could be fun, they were basically designed to be, but that was where it began and ended. Christmas was the only exception. Eggnog was part of it. Homemade and from scratch, with sprinkles of hand ground nutmeg dashed across the light-yellow surface. One sip could cure all that could be terrible about the world, at least for a moment. Even in the bleakness of early December, which was still technically late-autumn rather than winter, it could all make everything better. From the tree to the tinsel to the pudding no one really liked but pretended that they did. The magic of the season was down to tolerance, tradition and love. Until Halloween.

At the end of October, it hit like a brick. A mid-autumn shock that was not a treat or a trick, making any future holidays, even the holly-jolly, seem like a broken pencil. Pointless.

The autumn leaves had dropped, and the first flakes were expected to arrive by the week. Everything was made a bit blurry by rain in the meantime, any outdoor attempts at Christmas cheer put up since Thanksgiving sure to get drenched within seconds. Muzak renditions of Christmas classics chimed away in every mall from Seattle to Stockholm.

"Jiminy!" Heather yelped, as the tiny kitty going by the same name landed by her head to read over her shoulder.

Stepping down on the arm of the chair, the oddly green

kitten curled up on Heather's lap and purred herself to sleep. With a couple strokes of Jiminy's tiny head, Heather got back to the recently discovered exercise in fatuity.

Deep down in the dark depths of the trip booking rabbit hole, each site made even more ludicrous promises than the last, yet she kept falling for them. A hotel could promise an Olympic sized swimming pool, a kangaroo petting zoo and elephant rides and she would probably click just to see. Travel was, after all, an industry based entirely on profit and the desperation of city dwellers reaching their natural limit of concrete captivity, making for massive profits for those who can promise to get them out.

Heather's desperation only grew the more she knew about what a scam traveling could be. Fighting the urge to fall to her knees—Mr. and Mrs. Fideler had raised their only daughter to be a lot more dignified than that. She instead set her gaze skyward, appealing to a higher power.

"Please, just give me a sign!" she asked, not addressing anyone in particular.

Her request sent out to the universe, Heather got back to the computer, determined to give the little wheel on her mouse one last scroll before just hiding under the bed until it was all over.

A tiny island off the coast of her own city, settled by the Scots and known for its scenery and isolation, appeared from below the bottom limits of the search window. The name of the place, written in a happy blue just above a picture of an old-fashioned pub, was Heather's Haven.

"That was rhetorical!" Heather said, again looking skyward.

Cynical as she might have become, to the point she was comfortably numb, even Heather didn't falter in taking a chance when it was given. Scrolling down to the booking part, she gave it a double click for good measure. A photo of the pub's proprietor came up at the top of the form. It was a moment before Heather's breathing, let alone heartbeat, returned to form. Finally at the bottom of the form, after leaving her body to a mad scientist and signing away her first born in the terms and conditions, Heather clicked the last icon. Seeing the sweet notice of success, she relaxed a bit. The panic of packing and actually getting to her destination could wait until it was time to leave.

A xylophone of gentle clicks and clacks ran up Heather's back as she stretched to nearly twice her height, literally reaching for the sky as *Social Distortion* were imploring her to do just that on the wireless earbuds that were rarely out of her head.

"Coffee," Heather declared, getting up from the rolling office chair.

Banging like a drummer through every cupboard and cabinet housed in the mammoth kitchen that took up roughly a quarter of the main floor, Heather came up with nothing. Not a bean or ground to be found, even of the instant crystal variety. Gagging a little at the very thought, she deposited the little cat in her basket and set out into the icy December rain, desperately seeking relief.

Disguised as much as she could be by a hat and medical style mask, Heather walked into the relative warmth of the cafe, the smell of a dozen different grounds thick in the air.

Head down past the admirable attempts at cheering things up with lights and holly and such, the music mercifully better than most places that time of year, Heather got in line with the rest to wait her turn.

One of the weirdest things about her lot in life was being treated differently, despite the ideals of humility and respect being instilled in her from a young age. No one was essentially better than any other, no matter the evidence to the contrary. Corporate raiders, presidents, and kings ate, cried and died just like everyone else.

"Hey, sorry about this, but aren't you Heather Fideler?" the barista asked.

"Yes," Heather said, not wanting to be rude.

Most heads turned as the whisper ran around the cafe like a sugar-addled toddler. Unable to keep from rolling her eyes, Heather was losing any faith in her skills for disguise.

Stay calm, it's really just a part of the job. Heather took a table to wait for her order, taking requests for photos and autographs as gracefully as she had been instructed by her agents. Not even able to get coffee without attracting a bit of a crowd was simply the lot of the pop star. Even so, part of her looked forward to going somewhere with no Wi-Fi where she probably wouldn't be recognized, at least for a while.

Chapter Two: Kitten in the Basket

It looked like a life-sized game of *Tetris*. Her rolling upright suitcase lay open on the bed, ready to be loaded with all the essentials. Light packing had been handed down through generations of the Fideler family.

The rolling maneuver had come from Heather's mother, every outfit piled by size and then carefully rolled tightly into a tube, making for easier packing. Each log lay just right in the limited space, allowing her to fit in two to three times more than other, less efficient packing strategies. As she was the kind of girl who liked to have something to wear for every occasion, it was a relief.

Jiminy mewed from the bed, peeking into the top of her wicker style carrier, less a kennel than a wicker basket with a roof. The little kitty never seemed to mind being put in there, especially if it meant she got to come along.

"Jiminy!" Heather hollered, as the lid on the suitcase slammed closed.

To the sound of tiny and muffled mews, Heather lifted the lid, and Jiminy popped up like a jack-in-the-box looking a little out of sorts.

"You should probably stay out of the way," Heater said, placing Jiminy on the pillows.

Trooping back over to the basket, teeny Jiminy was peeking back in through the open top in no time.

"Okay, in you go," Heather cooed, giving Jiminy a boost into the basket, the itty-bitty kitty already having made it most of the way.

With happy mews of adventure, Jiminy was carried along with the suitcase out of the house and into the early morning, where the taxi waited.

"No pets," the cabbie said.

"There is for me," Heather said, giving him a grip of bills.

"Yes, Ms. Fideler!"

She thought he might salute before he loaded the suitcase into the trunk as she retreated into the backseat with the basket. There was no particular reason to have a car in a city like that. Parking was at a premium, and there really were easier ways of getting around.

The cab glided through the city as if the traffic didn't exist, the cluster of hustle and bustle falling behind them as the cab carried her to something more like sanity.

Brine filled Heather's nose, the smell of the sea making itself known before she could actually see it.

"Another ten minutes, Ms. Fideler," said the driver, in his thick Scottish brogue.

The ferry was nowhere near the dock when they arrived. There was probably some time before she would be able to get on anyway.

Paying the meter as it stood, Heather took her case and Jiminy down the ramp past the few cars waiting to get on, finding the bench set aside for walk-ons to wait. She checking her watch. With no schedule to be seen, her guess was as good as any on how long the ferry might be.

Spying a guy wearing a ferry sort of uniform on the other side of the gate that separated the loading ramp from the rest of the tiny terminal, Heather took a risk.

"Can I help?" he asked, not sounding at all put out.

"I sure hope so. Do you know when the next ferry leaves?"

"Well, it's about a three hour round trip on a good day. One left a while ago, so I'd say two hours or so."

"Okay, thank you," Heather said, her heart sinking into her

stylish but comfortable boots.

She had been a Doc Martens girl in her youth, but then the company sold out, getting the once-beautiful boots made for cheap in China. Heather had likewise defected to Australia and Blundstones, still made in Tasmania, as they'd been since Victoria was on the throne of England.

Faced with the fact of a long wait, she retired to the bench by the gate, accepting the not terrible fate. If that was as bad as things were going to get, at least that day, she was golden.

If a watched pot never boiled, an expected time never came. The digits on her phone screen changed as often as the full moon was seen, at least so it seemed.

Checking the battery on her trusty machine, she switched the playlist to something more upbeat and set things to shuffle, so each new track would be a surprise.

More cars came to silence after their roar as they took a place in line. It soon became clear many weren't going to make it on the next sailing.

"Excuse me, sorry but–"

"Yes," Heather said, expecting the rest.

"Yes?"

"I am Heather Fideler."

"Who?"

"You don't know me?"

"Uh, no, I don't believe I do. Have we met?"

"Not yet," Heather said.

"Well, I'm Aurora Bell," she said, offering a hand.

"Charmed."

Generally, the phrase was one of the more tell-tale signs of Heather's rampant Anglophilia. It had taken a single student trip to London for the essence to seep into her soul like a thick and refreshing fog. She'd even started taking tea, a habit that lasted more than a year after her return until her manager said she was getting fat.

It was only five pounds, but every ounce counted in a business like theirs, as much to do with the image as the sound going into the listeners ears. It was a sad reality of the universe, ever since the Fab Four first started wearing matching black suits and mop-top hairdos.

"See? Now we've met," Aurora said.

"Indeed," Heather agreed.

"Oh, kitty!" Aurora said, like she was five-years-old.

"Her name is Jiminy."

"Jiminy! Of course it is, she looks like a Jiminy."

"And acts like one too. It was the first thing my husband said when I got her."

"Your husband sounds neat," Aurora said.

"Yeah, he was."

Aurora didn't seem to notice the past tense, continuing to peep at little Jiminy through the gaps in the basket. The kitty was similarly taken.

"I think she likes me."

"Wouldn't surprise me, she likes everyone," Heather said.

With Aurora distracted by Jiminy, Heather occupied her mind by double checking her booking, her father's German side coming out in force.

"Oh, I know him," Aurora said, alerted by Heather's gasp at the sight of Silas Bailey on the account replying to her booking.

"You do?"

"Heck yeah! Si is my cousin!"

Heather's stomach settled as her mind raged. Smelling the water, natural if not entirely clean, after the cement, steel and glass of where she'd so recently been was a shock to the system.

She didn't move from the spot, just in case something happened while she was gone. It wasn't likely Aurora would make off with Jiminy, but any number of other things could happen when her back was turned.

"I see it," Aurora said, like she's just spotted Santa Claus.

Aurora probably wasn't more than a few years younger than herself, but she had a level of innocent exuberance Heather couldn't help but find endearing. Was everyone in Heather's Haven like that? They had grown up without the net, after all.

One by one, the cars started in an unbreaking chain, moving forward at the direction of the deck crew waving around orange batons like the ones used to direct planes on the runway.

When the last car was on, a separate, smaller gate opened near the bench, granting access to the walk-ons.

The commute was by far the worst part of travel. Whoever had the nerve to say getting there is half the fun was a liar, an idiot or a masochist.

Out on the mostly open deck of the pint-sized vessel, Heather took shelter from the sudden wind in a viewing port made in a side wall, while Aurora scampered to one of the passenger lounges.

The signs were clear that Heather wasn't allowed in there, at least with Jiminy, even though the permission signs all showed a dog to stand for all pets, which struck her as a little bit prejudiced.

Zipping up the padded wax jacket designed for traipsing across the chilly and treacherous Scottish moorlands, Heather did her best to shield Jiminy's basket from the worst of the wind with her suitcase. An hour and a half of standing wasn't Heather's idea of jolly rollicking fun, but at least she was finally on her way.

CHAPTER THREE: HEATHER'S HAVEN

No signal. Try as she might, that was all Heather's phone would indicate. It didn't even have the decency to show bars, allowing some hope, doomed as it might have been. Those two fatal words stayed stubbornly in the upper left corner of the screen. No Wi-Fi was one thing, but no phone service? It was getting downright medieval.

An optimist might try to look on the bright side — at least there wouldn't be the usual distractions while she was there, and there was no way for anyone to look her up or spread the word.

"Gang way," sounded the warning from behind, as a handful of lycra-clad cyclists zipped by on machines that probably cost as much as her best guitar.

Jiminy mewed her discontent, and Heather fought the urge to shake her fist at what she'd already decided must have been visiting city types, just like her. Was there no way to truly escape them?

Letting the cat out of the basket, Heather zipped her up inside her jacket, Jiminy's little kitty head peeking out above the zipper.

Nigel Partridge ran the only cab company on the island with himself and his son, Sonny Jim, as the only drivers of their pair of specially built vehicles. Left with no way to contact him, despite the number listed on the booking site, there was nothing to do but wait and hope he would show up before nightfall.

Had there been the usual dumping of the white stuff on the

little island as in the city, Heather would have been robbed of the view that greeted her as she sat on her reinforced suitcase. Resigned to her fate of a possibly long wait, she found everything taking on a sort of Zen quality after a while.

Just under a ten miles across in any direction, Heather's Haven was set on a bed of sedimentary rock that predated the dinosaurs. It was an expanse of grass clustered by forests here and there, reaching from one end to the other in any direction you cared to go, except where the land had been cleared intentionally so people could live more comfortably.

Immune to much of the weather that could be so cruel to the mainland, Heather's Haven was in just the right position, to remain moderate most of the time. There were patterings of rain and scatterings of snow, but it never lasted long, the land soon returning to its natural state. The heather plants for which it had been named came back en masse, turning the undeveloped and unfrosted segments to a waving sea of purple and green.

It wasn't the smell as much as the sight that struck Heather Fideler to the core. Gently sweet and naturally clean as the unmown grass, tiny purple plants swayed everywhere.

The honk shocked Heather back to reality as the taxis came along the slightly makeshift road at a sensible speed.

"You must be Heather," Nigel Partridge said.

"And you must be Mr. Partridge," Heather answered back.

It wasn't just the fact that he was behind the wheel of a cab that clued her in. Nigel Partridge was by far the most cabbie looking cabbie Heather ever saw. He was even wearing a khaki bomber jacket and gray tweed flat cap.

"Please, call me Nigel," he replied.

Out of the taxi with a spring in his step, Nigel put her suitcase into the trunk.

"Packing light, eh?" he asked, picking up the empty basket.

"Not exactly," Heather said as Jiminy made an appearance.

"Oh, hello little one," Nigel said, scratching the kitty behind the ear, much to Jiminy's delight.

"Does she have to ride in the trunk?" Heather asked, afraid the answer might be yes.

"Oh, goodness no, she'll be up front with us."

"That's allowed?"

"I say what's allowed in my cabs, love."

Nigel got into the driver's side, definitively bringing an end to it. Heather smiled despite herself, unaccustomed to such gentle authority and casual kindness.

With Heather belted into the passenger seat, Jiminy still in her jacket, cozy and purring, the cab left the dock behind, heading into the town proper.

"How did all the heather get here?"

"By the ferry, I would expect."

"No, I mean the plants, they're everywhere."

"Oh yeah, that. Bit of an odd story. Most think it goes back to Heather MacDonald, one of the first brave souls to set foot on our little piece of creation. Things were worse back home, or so the story goes. She came here for a new life. She always loved the heather growing all over the moors in those parts and snipped a bit to take with her. Most thought she was mad, and it would be dead by the time she got here."

"But it wasn't, was it?"

"No, indeed," Nigel confirmed. "It was every bit as hearty when she got to the island as when she'd first picked it. The first thing she did, even before building her settlement, was plant a bit of it. The nay-sayers were wrong about that too. Not only could heather grow here, but it also took to the land like a duck to water and spread like wildfire, only a lot less destructive."

"Is that why it's called Heather's Haven? Because Heather MacDonald found safety here?"

"Maybe. Either that, or the fact the native Scottish plant

took to another land so well. That's the odd part of the story, duckie. No one is quite sure which one it is."

Rain began to pitter-pat on the windshield and windows as the day waned, going from an overcast gray to a darker shade of blue. Jiminy hissed at the attacking water as was only appropriate. The only solace Heather could take was that it would have been snow almost anywhere else.

The village was dark, looking almost like a toy town by night when they arrived. Heather wondered if they ever filmed historical movies there. It would probably be pretty cheap, and the look and atmosphere were spot on. Had there been any citizens still on the narrow streets, she would have half expected them to be wearing gowns and ruffs, conversing jovially in iambic pentameter, taking the rustic chic ambiance to the third degree. Even beyond being outside the reach of Wi-Fi and cell-phone service. There was probably a switchboard somewhere on the island, connecting a network of landlines, where you put in number 1 to 150 or 200, according to who you wanted to reach.

Out the other side of what might well have been the only main street, the darkness of the natural landscape reasserted itself as the lights of town started to fade behind them. The headlights of the cab were the only light to be found as the wrath of the thunder god hammered down.

Just when Heather was beginning to worry she might have accidentally walked into a horror movie, another orange glow cut through the night up ahead, like a lighthouse on the dark sea.

Chapter Four: Bailey's Barley Barrel

Standing alone in the inky black, an old-fashioned single sign squeaked gently outside in a breeze off the sea, Bailey's Barley Barrel was the best chance for food and a place to sleep on Heather's Haven.

"I guess you don't have PayPal," Heather said, checking the meter.

"Nope."

Finding her wallet among the many pockets boasted by her wax jacket, rousing Jiminy in the process, she paid cash, the slightly rough feel of the bills a little strange on her fingers.

"Thank you kindly."

The suitcase and basket back on the ground, Nigel's taillights disappeared into the darkness like a ghost cab. Flighting a slight chill not from the weather, Heather popped the kitten back into the basket and approached Bailey's front door. Her way was lit by what was once an oil lamp, the casing having been updated to take a lightbulb instead.

Brass bells bonged overhead announcing their arrival. The deserted pub gave off a slightly haunted ambiance, as if Heather was the last surviving human.

"Hello."

"Gah!" Heather started, jumping about a foot straight up, setting Jiminy off hissing.

"Sorry, did I spook ya?"

"Just a bit," Heather said, trying to slow the pounding of

her heart.

"Oh, kitty!" the girl said, bending over to look in the basket. Jiminy let out a curious mew.

No more than twenty-two, the girl instantly reminded Heather of Aurora, confirming her theory there was something a little different about the island folk.

"I'm looking for Silas Bailey," Heather said, refusing to be charmed.

"Oh, you must be Heather."

"How do you know that?"

"I handle the bookings; Si is sweet but absolutely hopeless with anything invented after the 90s."

"Am I the only booking?"

"Yup, things wind down a bit during the off season. The Haven is more of a summer place, though I've never been sure why. It's practically perfect year-round, as far as I can tell."

Despite her somewhat grating exuberance, the girl certainly wasn't wrong about the nature of the place. The fact she would be the only guest took a load of Heather's mind.

"I'm Lily," said the kid, offering a hand.

"Lily Bailey?"

"Yeah."

"Sounds like a character in an old Romance novel," Heather said, a bit more bluntly than she meant.

"I suppose it does," Lily agreed, with characteristic generosity of spirit.

"Do I have to sign in or what?" Heather asked, getting things back on track.

"Oh, right, follow me."

Making the short trip to the bar counter, Lily heaved a huge leather-bound book up onto the oak surface. With an impressive efficiency, she flipped to a page with space, then produced a fountain pen out of the ether as far as Heather could tell.

The quill moved smoothly over the high-fiber paper, the black ink sinking in for posterity as Heather filled in her name and arrival date. The column for departure stood empty, leaving a wonderful sense of potentiality.

Her Blundstones thumping on the steps, Heather and Jiminy went upstairs, as per Lily's careful directions. She needn't have bothered, really, there were only six doors at the top of the stairs, each one marked by a brass number screwed into the heavy wood.

According to the registration book, Heather was put in room number two because it was the quietest. On the corner of the pub with two of its walls going to the outside and one out into the hall, with only the fourth connecting to another room, it was the farthest she could get from other people while still being in the building.

Heather's shoulders lowered by inches as the door closed behind her, finally getting where she most needed to be. Alone and away from it all, with nothing in the way of company except for sweet little Jiminy, the only one she could really stand to be around at the moment.

She opened the suitcase on the single bed with a bedspread that looked like it dated back to the 1920s, despite being nice and clean, and then unloaded the rolled clothes into the drawers of the dresser. Not having learnt her lesson back at the house, Jiminy saw something she thought needed attacking and pounced a bit too far before tumbling off the bed.

"Hey, are you okay?" Heather asked the dazed little kitty.

After a moment Jiminy recovered and started rubbing and purring in her hand. They both looked to the door as the knocks came, light and genteel. Exchanging a glance, Heather took Jiminy to see who their visitor might be.

"Hi," Silas Bailey said, holding a steaming mug of hot chocolate with little marshmallows floating on top.

"Oh, hi . . . oh . . . wha?"

A picture was one thing, but it didn't hold a candle to the real deal. The very fact of his presence, surrounding him like radio resonance, was enough to make her tongue stop cooperating.

Jiminy mewed at the potential intruder, managing to keep her wits about her, but the kitten was soon quelled by a scratch behind her ear.

"I thought you might like some hot chocolate," Silas said, taking the lead. "Kind of like a housewarming. A room warming, I guess."

"Thank you," Heather said, sounding about seven-years-old.

"Not a problem. Let me or Lily know if you need anything."

"Okay, thank you," Heather said, her adult tones returning after the initial shock.

The door closed with a heavy click, leaving Heather alone with Jiminy again. Absent-mindedly, she went back to the bed and took up the travel guitar cunningly hidden at the bottom of her suitcase. Attention was the last thing she wanted, and musicians tended to attract a lot, especially on ferries, as she'd found out in her early days.

Tuning up again after the day of travel, she got the strings sounding perfectly sweet once more and sat at the edge of the bed, facing away from the door.

With her fingers plucking the strings like they never had before, Heather wrote her first original song in years, every one of the words somehow rhyming with Silas. After getting through a good four stanzas and a bridge, the chorus yet to reveal itself, Heather remembered the hot chocolate, reminded by Jiminy who took to batting at the mug on the table just to see what happened.

"How did you get up there?" Heather asked the curious kitten, putting down the guitar to take Jiminy in one hand and the mug in the other.

Back on the bed, stroking Jiminy, Heather took a long sip of the sweet stuff which tasted like a bit of heaven in the Norman Rockwell mug.

CHAPTER FIVE: LIKE WALKING CATS

The heather stretched out as far as the eye could see in every direction, swaying its purple-green waves on the salty breeze as Heather and Jiminy strolled along the narrow road.

It was a far cry from trying to herd cats, but having Jiminy on a leash still felt a little out of whack, even if the little kitty seemed to be taking to it pretty well. It was Heather's own fault really. She hadn't thought to bring a litter box, so she'd used a particularly strong length of ribbon from the decorations that festooned her rented room to tie around Jiminy's collar, just to keep her from getting into too much mischief.

A pretty good kitty, most of the time, Jiminy didn't seem much to mind. Curious as ever, she still investigated everything she could find between the pub and town.

Heather always thought of December as being winter, mostly because of the song *In the Bleak Midwinter* sung around that time. Only thing was, the tune was first conceived when the Twelve Nights tradition was still a thing, and Christmas ran from December 25th to January 6th. *In the Bleak Midwinter* was usually sung around the time of Twelfth Night — not the Shakespeare play, but the historical tradition it was based on.

The temperature stayed consistent, Jack Frost nowhere near her nose. The refreshing cool kept her braced for the hike ahead. There had been a thought, or two, about calling Nigel back to get her, but the town really hadn't seemed so far in the dark.

Upon arriving at the first buildings of the tiny town in the middle of the small island, Heather noticed all of the architecture was built in an endearing Tudor style. Jiminy started to mew most pitifully, the cold and exercise getting to her.

"Okay then," Heather said.

Back in the wax jacket, Jiminy was still brave enough to peep out the top and watch the world go by, her irrepressible curiosity not to be defeated.

Despite the daylight, most of the shops, all of them also houses with living space up top, were shut. Even the library, which also had the town clock tower as part of its design, had a couple hours left before its opening time.

The only places that were open on either side of the street, separated by the red brick town square, were the bakery and the convenience store.

The bakery was clear where it stood on pets, which only made sense with all the raw ingredients around, and Heather didn't hold much hope for the corner shop.

"You look like you could use some coffee," the shopkeeper said, popping her head out as Heather and Jiminy passed by.

"I could, indeed," Heather agreed.

"I've got an espresso machine," the shopkeeper tempted.

"And I have a cat," Heather said, patting Jiminy on the head.

"Looks more like a kitten to me," the shopkeeper said, squinting close to the kitty. "Then again, so do I, maybe they could play together."

"Worth a try," Heather said, with a shrug.

Jangling through the door of the shop, she saw there was indeed a big orange cat in a basket behind the counter. Unzipping her jacket, Heather put Jiminy down on the floor so she could explore the immediate area around the other kitty.

"See? They're getting along already."

From what Heather saw, the older cat was mostly ignoring Jiminy as she bounced around like a jackass, which was probably for the best.

As promised, the espresso machine rumbled and hissed, Heather was glad there was a place to get decent coffee, not having thought to bring any of her own from home, a serious oversight that only indicated her frazzled state of mind when she made the booking.

A hum of pure contentment escaped her as she took that first perfect sip, the chemicals hitting her brain in all the right ways.

The bells rang again, putting Heather on high alert. Grabbing Jiminy, who let out a surprised little mew, she ducked into a side aisle, not really wanting to meet anyone new if she didn't have to. Heather was nothing if not pragmatic.

"Well, Finty Foss," she could hear the shopkeeper greet the new arrival.

"Hello, Agnes."

"How are things in the newspaper trade?"

Heather backed up a little more. The media had been both the best and the worst thing for her life and career over the last decade or so.

"Can't complain, especially not with who was seen coming over on the ferry!"

"Oh? And who might that be?"

"Are you ready for this?" Finty asked.

"Probably not but go ahead."

"Heather Fideler."

"Who?" the shopkeeper asked.

"You know, the Pop Star. Aurora saw her at the ferry terminal."

"Nope, sorry the name doesn't ring a bell. Heather Fideler, I mean, not Aurora."

In addition to no Wi-Fi and no phones, aside from the local landlines run by the central switchboard, Heather's Haven apparently didn't have much in the way of tabloid newspapers. There certainly weren't any in the shop.

"What do I owe you?" Heather asked when Finty Foss was safely gone.

"Not a thing, dear."

"Oh, thank you! Are you sure? I'm rich you know."

"Are you? How nice dear, yes, I am quite sure."

Out into the cool morning once more, none other than Silas Bailey came down the street. Ducking into the stationary store, Heather browsed the leather brown notebooks and fountain pens until the coast was clear.

"Can I help you?" asked the clerk, not in an unfriendly way.

"Um, yes please, uh, I'll take these," Heather said, holding up the nearest pad and pen, which rang up to a combined cost of nearly a hundred dollars.

Chapter Six: Kittys and Cocoa

On a dead and dreadful December day, Heather Fideler remained locked behind the hefty oak door of her room at the pub. Jiminy ran about like a jungle cat, up over the bed and then under before for taking a quick break and shooting off again for another lap around.

On the island of Heather's Haven, things had set into a more wintery way. Far from the dumping expected in the city, even the snow was gentle, sprinkling the world in light flakes, like putting a pinch of nutmeg on top of eggnog.

Back into town, Heather went to see what she could see, finding an impressively popular library. Less a book depository than a community center, the place was always hopping. Not just with those looking for something new to read, but just about every club in town had their meetings in the back room of the small building, at least two such gatherings happening every day, according to the notices taped to the door.

In her wanderings with the little cat, Heather had learned a lot about the odd place so close and also so far from everything she knew. Despite serious attempts to try and keep her head down, she had already been recognized once. Even if it was by fluke, it couldn't happen again.

Aurora didn't seem to know who she was at the ferry terminal. In fact, she'd flatly said so. The girl was so sweet and literal, Finty could have just asked about her day, and Aurora would say she had met Heather Fideler. Despite not knowing who that was.

No matter the reason, lies or literalism, Heather knew it

could not happen again.

She was just one misplaced word from being discovered, making Heather's Haven just one more place she couldn't be. She had gone there to be alone, and it would probably be best if she stuck with that original plan.

It wasn't all bad. She hadn't been truly alone in a while. It wasn't just on account of the fans, recognizing her wherever she went, but the whole ecosystem of management, media, promotion and lackeys that had grown up around her and her *brand*, entire teams of women and men dedicated to getting her noticed in a good way so, at the end of the day, they could all get paid.

It wasn't a bad life, in a way. The money was nice, especially after so long a struggle, never starving, but well aware of what it was like to have not quite enough. At the very least, she didn't have to worry about the rent being late. The only problem was it wasn't her life anymore. Almost every hour was planned by her managers and label.

For a while, the first few years, at least there was the music, the thing she loved most and wanted to share with the world. That balm made the harsh reality of the industry easier to take, at least in the beginning. By album number three, every note and word had been written by legacy songwriters who'd penned hits for some of the biggest names in the game before Heather was even born. She was both too early and too late but refused to be a victim of fate.

On the bed of the pub rental, legs crossed like she'd done back in college, she plucked at her travel guitar as though it was the vintage Martin that had cost more than her first car. She'd left that one at home in hopes of anonymity.

Notes drifted into the small space as they blended and harmonized, first with each other and then with her voice as she improvised lyrics, to be written down on the pad beside her with the new purchased fountain pen, to be edited into something like a final form later.

"Jiminy!" Heather shouted, as the knocks came on the door. The itty-bitty kitty obediently jumped up on the bed. "No, not you honey."

Raised far too well to leave a visitor waiting, Heather scratched the kitten behind her ear and answered the door.

"Hello!" Lily Bailey chirped sweetly.

"Um, hi?" Heather asked, it being the first word that came to her.

"Was that you playing?"

"Sure as heck wasn't Jiminy," Heather said, as the kitty took the cue to rub around Lily's legs, purring to high heaven.

Lily scratched Jiminy behind the ear, careful with the mug of cocoa she was holding in her small but sturdy hand with its little marshmallows bobbing on the top,

"I think she likes me," Lily said as Jiminy mewed in agreement.

"She likes everyone."

"Unlike you?"

Had she been anyone else, the question would have been pointed enough to make Heather bleed. The younger of the Bailey siblings had enough sweet curiosity in her inquiry to make it almost endearing.

"Something like that," Heather said, more honest than she'd been in a while.

"Oh, okay, I was going to ask if you might like to play at our open mic night, but that might not be a good idea. Cocoa? Si made it himself."

"Yes."

"To cocoa?" Lily asked.

"Both," Heather said, before she could stop herself.

CHAPTER SEVEN: I HAVE NO WORDS

Heather sat on the bed like she did in the old days when the less time spent in the three-hundred dollar an hour studio, the better. Maximum output for the least amount of time, or money, was the brutal efficiency of the record industry, rather removing much of the passion and fun of music making.

As Heather played, Jiminy was engaged in some serious business, keeping an eye on a fly that had found its way into their space. Her little head darted around in a way that made Heather wonder how the kitty didn't get dizzy.

Heather finalized the last verse of her third new song. The page was a mess of red and blue felt-tip revisions. The travel guitar was more a matter of fitting the words to the melody. Unlike the stereotype of Pop Stars, Heather was well aware of her syllable count. Her first love was not a musician, in the traditional sense, but a poet—Shakespeare.

The sonorous music in each and every line stirred her heart and gripped her mind like little else, especially in terms of the comedies. *Much Ado About Nothing* was a particular stand-out. She'd wanted to call her first album *Benedick & Beatrice* but the suits at the label didn't get it and insisted on something more *accessible*, eventually going with *2 of Hearts*, including the incongruous numeral.

She might have complained at the time had she not already signed on the dotted line when she was all of eighteen. It wasn't quite in blood, befitting the Faustian mode, but it had begun started to seem that way pretty quick. Getting everything she thought she wanted, not at the cost of her soul, but certainly her spirit, which was nearly as bad, on balance.

As she cracked her back, a slight sigh of sweet relief escaping her lungs, a knock came on the door.

"Hi!" Lily said.

"Hello," Heather said, taking a slight step back where it was safe.

"We'll be starting in about thirty minutes. You're near the top of the list, so it would be good if you were down there when we start."

"Okay. Say, you wouldn't know how to get a kitten out from under a bed would you?"

"Have you tried catnip?" Lily asked.

"Fresh out."

"Tuna?"

"Didn't think to bring any."

"Wait here."

Dashing downstairs for two minutes, Lily returned with a can of beans and a manual can opener.

"I don't think she likes beans," Heather observed.

"Just watch."

Setting the can in the opener, Lily gave it three good twists, Jiminy busting out from her hiding place at speed, bouncing slightly off Lily's shins before rubbing around her legs, purring up a storm.

"How?" Heather asked.

"All cans sound the same to a cat."

"Won't she be disappointed?"

"Probably, she'll soon forget, just give her lots of cuddles and love."

"Okay."

"After your set, of course," Lily said, picking up the affectionate kitty.

"Right, of course," Heather said, going for her guitar.

After they went downstairs together, Lily left the can of beans with Silas to take back into the kitchen before sitting in the assembled crowd.

The tables in the barroom at Bailey's Barley Barrel had been moved off to the sides, all the chairs set up in rows in front of a make-shift stage set-up at the west wall with a stool and with two microphones, one for voices the other for instruments, connected to an aged PA system. The entire rig was run from a table off to the right.

It was probably impossible, but it looked like everyone in town was there, most of the chairs probably already occupied by the time Lily had come to get her with just under half an hour to spare.

Heather hadn't played a pub gig in nearly a decade, but it all soon came back to her, including the crushing fear. Small, intimate spaces where you could see everyone's faces were much more intimidating than a dark sea of fans, barely distinguishable from the stage of a stadium. All she was likely to see when facing the crowd at Bailey's Barely Barrel were dozens of locals waiting. Expecting. Judging.

"Cranberry juice, please," Heather said, physically leaning on the bar for support as most of the strength fled from her knees.

"Sure, you okay?" Silas asked.

"Oh, yeah, of course, just slightly terrified is all."

"You don't say."

"Just did."

"I suppose it wouldn't help to imagine everyone in their underwear."

"No, probably not," Heather replied, after some serious thought. She downed three cranberry juices in as many minutes.The natural acid burned Heather's belly as it sharpened her mind, in the nick of time.

"Heather," the producer said, reading off the list.

Her head lower than she ever thought it could go, the flat cap pulled down well over her eyes, Heather made her way through the crowd. They couldn't see her if she couldn't see them. Sometimes ignorance really was bliss.

"Get a compound fracture!" Lily encouraged, giving an adorable thumbs up as Heather glanced back at her.

Peeking up from under her cap, risking a glance at the crowd and instantly regretting it, Heather spotted Finty sitting near the center of the fourth row, because *of course* she was.

Scrapping all the lyrics she'd spent hours on, her voice far too distinctive not to be a dead giveaway, Heather went into an instrumental medley of her newest compositions, making them sound like a single continuous song with distinct movement—one that managed to get a standing ovation from the already receptive audience of islanders and fellow visitors.

CHAPTER EIGHT: AN INCIDENTAL TOURIST

Local sparrows held choir practice outside the window, and the smattering of snow was chased away by a dampening rain that rarely got past a drizzle. The cautious calm had returned the day before, Heather's Haven boasting one of the mildest climates in the world, which went a ways to explain why people chose to live there full time despite the utter lack of Wi-Fi.

Dancing pajama-style to the dresser, Heather got out her second-to-last outfit, noticing the immediate need for clean laundry.

There had been someone around to do almost everything for her since Heather was nineteen when her second album hit big, but Heather still had slightly misty memories of her mother showing her how to set a washing machine, sure it would all come back when she was confronted with one, like riding a bike. Alternatively, she could probably just pay Lily or someone to do it for her when it came down to it.

Such a sly solution was definitely better for her plan of going unnoticed. She'd been pretty lucky to that point, but it couldn't last forever. The less time she spent in public, no matter how pretty or friendly the town, the better. Even though it was kind of nice, just for a change, not to be constantly stalked by hunters with cell phones.

"Jiminy!" Heather started as the knock came on the door.

In rather more of a friendly mood, Jiminy scurried to reply, mewing encouragement as Heather lagged behind.

"Good morning," Silas said, as Jiminy did her usual rubbing and purring dance around his legs.

It is now! Heather thought, already lost in his eyes. If she didn't get out soon, she might never be found.

"Need something?" Heather asked, looking down.

"Only to tell you that breakfast is ready, if you want it."

"I didn't order breakfast."

"In-house service for our long-term residents."

"Thank you," Heather said, not quite believing it herself.

"No trouble," Silas Abraham Bailey said with a smile that turned her knees to jelly.

In her best jeans and hoodie, going for a high-class casual look, Heather left Jiminy batting around one of her socks as she went down for breakfast.

"Good morning," Lily said, taking Heather in a hug.

"Good morning to you too," Heather said. She shot a slightly desperate glance to Silas, searching for some kind of explanation.

He could only shrug and shake his head, as if to say *that's our Lily.*

Able to breathe again, Heather headed for the well-set-up table with everything she liked the most laid on quaint but charming earthenware plates with carved and varnished wooden cutlery, a taste of the country in almost the literal sense.

Suspicion clashed with glee doing bloody battle on the field of Heather's mind as the ghost of a smile haunted her newly make-up free face.

She'd felt naked the first few times, but it seemed as good a disguise as any, like a man shaving his beard.

Wood scraped on wood as she ate, muffled sounds of comfort and joy coming out of Heather at regular intervals, whether she wanted them to or not.

"Good?" Silas asked, bringing her more cranberry juice.

"Spectacular," Heather blurted.

"Glad to hear it," Silas said.

He left her to eat in peace, and Heather nearly asked him not to go. There was no point in trying to be alone if she was going to swoon over every handsome man, but Silas was something else. She couldn't quite say what it was but was keen to find out.

The breakfast dishes cleared away, Heather was headed back up to her room, this time to stay, just to make sure her natural emotions couldn't be spurned. Her father's inexplicable love for the Buzzcocks was coming back again to bite Heather on the bum. Not quite in keeping with his public image, Nathan Fideler III often had near-mint vinyl pressings of some of the more melodic punk releases rotating on the turntable during much of Heather's rearing. The first song she ever learned on her dad's old Stella acoustic guitar with the rare steel tail-price was Joy Division's *Shadowplay*, much to her mother's dismay at one fateful school talent show.

Her slightly isolationist tendencies first showed when she was wee, a theme that continued through much of her life. A guidance counsellor at one of the many high schools she found herself attending said that Heather was far too young to be so jaded. She'd answered back, not a great idea at a private school, with chapter and verse of The Kinks *I'm Not Like Everybody Else*.

Her attitude had eventually softened with age and experience, going from a tears-on-the-diary-page depression to a more Absurdist view of life, the universe, and everything. So, she made sweet, catchy, melodically complex Pop Music because that was what people needed sometimes. Choosing not to live in denial of harsh reality or get frustrated or battered by it, she went with a third option, existing in defiance of it.

"Would you like me to show you around?" Silas asked, halting her exit.

"Sorry?"

"Around the island, I mean. There is a lot more to see. And some nooks and crannies you might not expect."

"Will there be a lot of people around?" Heather asked.

"No, none at all, really. Most of the two-legged creatures stay in town, going about their day. Where I'm thinking of going it will just be you, me and the sheep."

"Sheep?"

"On the farms," Silas explained.

"Farms?"

"We aren't going to get very far if you just keep repeating everything I say," he pointed out gently.

"Fair enough, but there are farms?"

"Yes, and fields."

"Noticed those, a little hard to miss, really."

"And forests and streams, all leading to the surrounding coast. The whole thing is pretty diverse, really."

"Sounds interesting," Heather had to concede.

"Well then, come and see."

The offer was tempting indeed, a day alone with Silas, surrounded by the island's natural beauty.

"I'll need someone to watch Jiminy."

"Cats are very independent."

"She's a *kitten*, and it isn't really *her* I'm worried about."

Silas rubbed his chin, considering the problem in a most sagely way.

"Lily could do it,"

"Won't she be busy?"

"What, with all these customers?" Silas asked, indicating the otherwise empty dining room.

"Point taken."

Leaving the sweet kitty in Lily's capable hands they set out into the wind, nearly matching wax jackets zipped up over their chins with the help of their teeth.

The engine at a low rumble, his truck carried them away from the pub as well as the town, the closest thing to civilization the island knew, aside from a few scattered houses on the farms, and cabins built in the smatterings of woods that came up here and there like patch-work.

No one bothered the few local hermits on Heather's Haven, aside from stopping by to make sure they were still well alive. Most could do what they wanted on that sweeping sea of purple and green, punctuated by buildings, farms and trees, usually raising no more than an *oh, aye* from other islanders.

As they got farther into the *out there* Heather's head was a little scared, but her heart was feeling free, just where she would want to be if ever given the option.

Rolling down the window, she let her hair fly around her as the wind whipped past, bracing against her face. She felt truly alive for the first time in years.

"That's the spirit," Silas said, as Heather let go a yell of thrilled exhilaration.

All too soon, stillness resumed as the truck rolled to a halt a little off the road to keep from making a hazard for others.

Everywhere she looked, Heather was surrounded, and not only by the swaying purple and green. There was a small forest to the right and a fenced off patch of farmland where dozy sheep grazed, knowing the grass from the heather.

Finding a good spot, Silas got out and led the way across the landscape, which was harder to cross than it first looked.

"Come on," Silas urged, trudging even farther, through the tall grass.

Secretly glad to be wearing pants, even on that rare sunny day, Heather trailed Silas through her namesake, a third sort of scenery making itself known as they got to the inevitable coast.

A sandy beach extended to the sparkling sea, which reached out as far as her eyes could see, meeting the sky at a certain, distant point.

"Shall we?" Silas asked.

"Shall we what?"

With the smooth charisma of a magician, Silas conjured an old-fashioned checkered picnic blanket from a wicker basket tucked casually over the arm Heather couldn't see. The blanket wafted to the heather and grass, spreading itself out perfectly over his chosen spot.

"Are you a warlock?" Heather almost accused.

"Not that I know of."

"Good, just checking."

Heather joined Silas on the blanket, the grass soft and cushy beneath, making things extra comfy as Heather tried to process everything going on around her.

"What did you bring in your pic-a-nic basket? Wine and Cheese?"

"Not exactly."

Showing being better than telling, Silas took out everything from the cans of local no-alcohol spritzer to the crackers and wheel of brie.

"Why are you psychic?" Heather asked suspiciously.

"What do you mean?" Silas asked, his mouth already full of crackers and cheese.

"How did you know everything I like?"

"I didn't. Lily packed the basket mostly for me, probably thinking there would be a few things you would like too."

"Try everything."

"No kidding."

"I never kid about picnics," Heather said, with all the gravitas of a Shakespearean tragedy.

"Duly noted."

Out of nowhere, the flakes came as they ate, the weather tending to turn on a dime. It was usually milder than average for the season, but rarely consistent from one day to the next.

The little island named after a pretty plant had gotten all the sunny days it was due and was in line for a perfectly season-able dump of snow that came around once every decade or so.

With characteristic stoicism, Silas packed everything up and headed back to the car as Heather went into a mild panic.

"We should get back before it gets worse," Silas said.

"Worse?" Heather asked, not at all comforted by his words.

With the widows up and the heater on, Silas piloted the pick-up toward the pub.

"Whoa!" Heather said, grabbing the emergency bar as the truck hit a rough patch on the road.

"It's okay," Silas said. "I've got snow tires on and we're al-most back."

She watched the flakes hit the windshield, tumbling to earth like their autumn counterparts, each adding to the mass already gathered.

If Heather ever needed a reason to stay in the pub a little longer, a snow-in was it. As long as they kept power and food, a week or so with Jiminy and the Baileys might not be so bad after all.

CHAPTER NINE: BAKER'S DOZENS

Heather patted Jiminy's head, the tiny kitty now secured in Lily's capable grasp. Every so often, from the time Heather was wee, the craving struck for something to be found in a bakery. The brighter and cuter the better. Something decorated with a teddy bear or the like rarely went amiss.

It was required entirely, the dependency more psychosomatic than physical. The doctors had been clear enough about that. But if she didn't get it, there was a chance she would get back to the edge of an abyss. There was something about sugar, even beyond the sweetness, that assisted her like nothing else.

The pang struck again as Jiminy let out a little mew, watching Heather go into the remains of the winter wonderland Heather's Haven had become. Silas was nowhere to be seen, but it didn't matter much in terms of Heather's plan. Nigel Partridge was already on his way, following the grooves left behind in the snow by Silas's truck.

Things had settled down quite a lot. There was enough snow on the ground in the undisturbed sections to come up to Heather's shins as she trudged through the path left by Silas to his truck.

There was no telling where he might have gone, just that he wasn't there a lot of the time. He left the pub, which was unlikely to see any more customers until spring, or at least the next open mic, in the care of his darling little sister. He must have trusted her a lot, but then Heather really wouldn't be one to talk. It was already the second time Heather had left Jiminy with the younger Bailey sibling.

"Morning," Nigel said, in his characteristically jovial way.

"Hi, Nigel."

"Where to?"

"The bakery."

"Right.

Taking the most direct route, and not only because it would be far too obvious if he hadn't, but the main road also only went north or south, Nigel soon had Heather back to the town square. In the fountain, the water remained still, shut off until the late winter thaw that tended to kick in on the island some-time around February.

"Want me to wait?" Nigel asked.

"Can you? With only the two of you, I mean."

"Sure, junior can handle any other fares, it should be a pretty slow day."

"Okay."

Secretly glad she wouldn't have to wait on the way back, Heather found a way over to the bakery, the heavenly smell hitting her as soon as she jangled through the door.

"Good morning!"

"Hi," Heather said, a little taken aback.

"What can I get you?"

The usual island friendliness had taken the bakers as well.

Searching the plethora of pockets in her waxed jacket, Heather found the list, laying it on the counter.

"For here or to go?" the clerk asked, reaching the bottom of the scroll-length series of requests.

"To go, in boxes, please."

"You have a car?"

"A taxi."

"Ah, same difference, Nigel or his boy?" the clerk asked.

"Nigel."

"Good. Tip him with a cupcake and he'll be your best friend."

Heather could do with a friend right about then and made a note of it. Even if she was already getting closer with Lily and would very much like to get to know Silas a lot better.

"Oh, hello," said a familiar voice from behind her.

A gentle heat rushed to her cheeks, as Heather tried her level best to find a way to answer.

"Hi," was all she came up with, coming out as a breath.

Not the coolest of impressions but it would do in a pinch. Vowing to do better, she waited for his response.

"Stocking up, hey?" he asked, as the clerk came back, a little obscured by the white take-out boxes tied up with twine.

"Yeah," Heather said, blushing even harder.

She didn't mind her little problem if as few people knew about it as possible. Back in the city she had people go and get such orders. So, of course, the first time she had to do it while on the Haven, it was Silas Bailey who spotted her. Murphy's Law was in full effect.

"Clever. It could be a while before the roads are really clear. You come in with Nigel?"

"Exactly," Heather said, agreeing with both his statement and his question.

"Need any help carrying things out?" he asked, sweetheart that he was.

"Yes, please."

Heather was just about to turn when another jingle sounded from the door, and it wasn't from sleigh bells either.

"Hello!" greeted an all too familiar voice in tones that sent icy spiders of dread scurrying up Heather's back.

Taking a quick, diversionary tactic, Heather veered over to one of the small tables as Finty made her-way to the counter to slightly terrorize the clerk for information.

"What are we doing?" Silas asked.

"Waiting," Heather said, doing her best to change her voice.

When Finty was good and distracted, asking the clerk if she'd seen or heard anything about Heather being there, Fideler and Bailey dashed for the door and out into the snow.

"What the heck was that about?" Silas asked.

"How much time do you have?"

After paying Nigel his due, Heather got a ride back to the pub with Silas. The added space of the truck came in handy in terms of loading the boxes of bakery goodness.

Seated at the table, her load already hidden in her room to avoid the cheek burning shame of her human frailty, Heather came clean.

"I'm famous," she said, the words sounding weird.

"Famous?" Silas quizzed.

"In the city—most cities, actually. No one here seems to know who I am. I'm guessing because of the whole no internet thing. I'm a musician, as you've probably guessed. I've put out six platinum selling albums and have a list of awards longer than my leg."

"Must be interesting," Silas said.

"Yeah, it was, not so much anymore. I'm here to try and get away from all that and . . . other things. Only thing is—"

"Finty knows," Silas said.

"Yeah."

"She is a journalist after all."

"So I hear. And I have to wonder how long it is going to be before everyone else knows, too, and it all starts up again."

CHAPTER TEN: PICTURE IT

Jiminy needed out and quick, making her demands known in a yowl that should've been beyond such a tiny cat, marching before the door like an agitated Major-General. She had only used a box for a month or so, and took to the walks with aplomb.

"Okay, okay," Heather surrendered, pushing back from the table.

Heather clipped on the little leash Lily helped her find, and Jiminy trotted along good as could be out onto the landing and down the creaking stairs into the pub proper.

"Oh, cute!" Lily gushed as the odd pair came down to the hardwood.

Jiminy glanced in the direction of the compliment and lifted her chin just a bit, as though to say *yes, I know*.

The snow remained, light and crisp, the rain that might turn it to slush staying well away. In Heather's humble opinion, slush was worse than snow, or even ice. There were no such problems in the Haven. The road held only a couple layers of tight packed snow, stained a surreal grey by car exhaust, the sort of shade that only happened by accident, organic sources of black and white finding each other in the course of a day.

Crisp but not cold through her wax jacket, Heather made the trek from the pub to town, Jiminy far more interested in bouncing between the road and the snow in the field, her little kitty paws light enough to let her run across the top of the snow banks.

Time could move differently when you weren't paying attention. In what felt like minutes, Heather could see the lights of main street, the town just waking up for the day.

"Fancy a coffee?" Heather asked Jiminy, bringing about a mew of agreement.

Getting Jiminy into one of the lower cargo pockets in her quite practical jacket, Heather jangled through the door of the corner shop.

"Hello again," Agnes sang.

"Coffee?"

"Of course."

The machine set off humming and steaming like something invented by a Victorian mad scientist, Heather eventually getting the goods in a lidded take-out cup.

"Perfect," Heather said, after the first blissful sip.

"Glad to hear it."

Paying the piper, as according to the ancient warning, Heather turned to leave, having met her requirements for the day.

"There you are!"

Heather glanced back at Agnes, who shrugged.

"You're Heather, right?"

"I am."

"We have to talk," the stranger said.

"Pretty sure we already are," Heather said.

"Alone."

"You mean without witnesses?" Heather asked.

"No."

"You might want to tell your face."

"I look—intimidating?" the stranger asked.

"As Lady Macbeth on a bad day."

"My apologies. I would like to keep things civil."

"Too late," Heather observed.

"Fine, I'll just come out with it shall, I?"

"Yes," Heather invited.

"I need you to stay away from Silas."

"Silas Bailey?"

"That's the one."

"That might be difficult, considering I am staying at his pub."

"Not what I meant."

"What do you mean?" Heather asked.

"Just stay away from him, okay? He has enough to deal with without getting into that whole mess again."

"I guess that depends."

"On what?" The stranger asked.

"Who are you?"

"Someone who doesn't want to see him get hurt again."

"What the heck was that about?" Heather asked, when the estranged had jangled back out the door.

"Betty can be quite passionate," Agnes said.

"Betty?" Heather asked, instantly thinking of Betty Boop.

"Betty Highsmith."

The only Highsmith Heather knew about was Patty, but Betty didn't look much like her. Far too hard and angular. The long-dead author always had more of a soft baby face. Betty could stun a rampaging rhino at fifty yards with a glance.

"She's . . . intense."

"All bark, darling. She's just trying to protect him, pay no mind."

Silas seemed so together; it was difficult to imagine him having problems at all. You never really knew what was going on with someone else.

"What happened?" Heather asked.

"I think that's for him to tell, dear. Though you should probably know he's much better now, and Betty is being a little bit silly. "

"Good to know."

The coffee was still steaming, giving a much needed shot of caffeine for the trek back to the pub.

Jiminy started shivering halfway back to their toasty warm room, the cold finally getting to her. Tucking the kitty into the front of her padded jacket, Heather trudged back to where she needed to be.

"Good morning," came a familiar voice from behind the truck.

Peeking around the side, just to see what she might find, Heather found a very strange sight.

Sitting at an easel, a steaming coffee on a stool beside it, sat Silas, in little more than jeans and a Merino sweater, painting a photo-realistic rendering of the scene behind the pub. The white expanse of the snow matched that of the blue sky until it dropped off the coast into the ocean. White and blue changed to blue on blue in the distance, or so it looked, going by the perspective he was using.

CHAPTER ELEVEN: COME FROM AWAY

The brush flowed across the set canvas like a skater on a lake as each stroke left its mark, turning the once-blank space into a work of art before her eyes. She'd seen painters in the park back in the city, doing landscapes and the like but never anything like that.

"That's really good," Heather blurted.

"I try," Silas replied, with the honest modesty of the truly gifted.

The brush continued to create the composition out of nowhere, like it was a magician's wand conjuring the image, making a new reality.

"Where did you learn?"

"London."

"You don't have an accent," Heather blurted.

"Don't I? Oh dear, I have been here a while."

"Here?"

"Heather's Haven. The dialect is one of the many unique things around here."

"I thought you grew up here."

"Lily did, much by my design. I don't think she remembers anything . . . before."

His expression changed, letting Heather know that no matter how much she might want to, it was better not to ask. Heather's Haven wasn't a place you ended up by accident. You were either born there, brought there, or got there as the result of special effort. That was probably why the islanders could be so friendly. They recognized another escapee when they saw one.

"Where did you go to school? The institution I mean."

"Oh, the Royal Academy."

Of course, it was somewhere amazing like that. Silas was so impressive there was nowhere else it could be. He probably had pieces hanging in the Tate Modern and won a Turner Prize, or a better one, before giving it all up to relocate to that primitive but lovely little island.

"You gave it all up?"

"I don't see it that way," Silas said, dabbing in the seagull that decided to fly by, captured in oil on canvas for the rest of time.

"It wasn't a sacrifice?"

"More of a change. I still paint and people still see them, it's just on a smaller scale with less pomp and history. A fine exchange for a peaceful life and a safe place for Lily to grow up."

"How old was she when you came to here?"

"Five. She's twenty-one now. Far as she knows, we've always been here."

"How old are you?" Heather blurted.

"Thirty-eight. I know, I don't look it, family curse."

"Seventeen years between you?" Heather asked, doing the math on her fingers.

"Indeed, you could say she came as something of a surprise, but a wonderful one."

"Where are your parents?"

It was a question that gnawed like a goblin at the back of her mind since meeting the slightly eccentric siblings. Both of them were, technically, adults, but it struck her as odd that didn't have family around.

"France, now. They wanted to retire early and thought coming here was a good idea. Hung about for a decade or so, until Lily was older. Dad helped me buy this place. When Lily was fifteen they asked if she wanted to go with them to Calais and she nearly cried."

"Got used to island life, hey?"

"And how."

"Do you ever think about leaving?" Heather asked.

"Sometimes, old habits, I guess. Then I remember that I have almost everything I could ever want or need right here."

"Almost?"

"Never managed to get married. Always thought I would . . . eventually."

It was the first time Heather Fideler witnessed anything like sadness in Silas Bailey's bearing.

Only the swish of the brush and whisper of the wind were left as Silas finished off the painting, perfectly picturing the scene in front of them, as though he was afraid he might forget.

Dipping a fine-tip brush, almost like a pen, into a blob of sable black on the ceramic pallet, Silas signed his name at the bottom right, the letters sweeping and looping together in a practiced way.

"We should head inside," Silas said. "It is only going to get colder."

Jiminy mewed her agreement from inside Heater's jacket. Taking up the canvas by the crossbar and folding it and the paint box under his arm, Silas sauntered toward the pub as fresh flakes started to sprinkle the island.

Silas headed toward a side door in the empty barroom Heather had never noticed before, set next to one of the booths along the east wall.

"I have more, if you want to see," Silas invited.

Shifting the kitty back to her pocket, Heather unzipped her jacket and followed Silas through the semi-secret passage.

"Close your eyes," Silas said, as he flicked on the light, the space going from pitch dark to light.

As her vision cleared, Heather peered into the Bailey studio. Both small and yet large enough, every inch of available space was used to its ultimate potential.

Along the back wall canvases stood, lined up single-file. Others, not quite dry enough to join the main collection, were lined up on a shelf built into the wall above it. Silas added the most recent composition to the shelf, assessing the position and angle before letting it go.

"They're great," Heather said.

"Thank you."

"Seriously, I don't know if they are paintings or windows."

"I doubt that, but honestly, thank you."

"Better be careful, or Finty might be after you for an interview," Heather joked.

"Finty is after you, hey? I suppose it was bound to happen eventually."

"How so?"

"You're famous right?"

Heather's heart dropped into her stomach, her face feeling like it had gone from mocha to off-white, as the blood drained away.

"I used to be. Does anyone else know?" she asked, trying to keep her voice even.

"Doubt it. Finty can get a bit obsessed, always looking for a good story. She basically runs the paper and sees it as her duty."

"Oh."

"Most folk around here wouldn't know what she was on about anyway, even if she did spill the beans. Much like with the phone, the newspaper really only exists on the Haven."

Chapter Twelve: Head Held High

It was done. The jury in Heather's head, the one that had been there for her earliest memories, had come to a verdict, and it was unanimous. She was going to make herself known to the islanders of Heather's Haven, tell the whole truth and let any consequences go hang. She had lived a lie for far too long.

At the table directly across from the bed, where Jiminy brought her usual mischief, Heather did her level best to get into a calm and peaceful state of mind.

Not quite able to manage the lotus position, she did her best with crossed ankles and closed eyes. Her grandmother had sworn by meditation, mostly because George Harrison had.

Finding her third-eye firmly shut, even more than the two obvious ones, Heather made do with some good old-fashioned *oms* and deep cleansing breaths, which seemed to do the trick.

"Right," she said, convincing herself as much as the invisible jury.

Bundled up as well as she could manage, Heather thumped down the stairs with a slightly startled Jiminy in her pocket.

"Heading out?" Lily asked.

"I am."

"Can I watch Jiminy?" the younger Bailey asked, before Heather could make the request.

"Sure, if you insist."

Old snow sparkled with prisms of rainbows, and the road had once again pounded down to something flat and safe. The snow on Heather's Haven, when it came, did so with no threat of rain. It was one or the other, making ice something that happened to other people. Walking with an upright confidence, Heather crossed the space between pub and town faster than ever. Not even breaking a sweat before she spied the red-brick clock tower reaching into the clear island sky.

Her face braced by what wind there was, it was the first time Heather had been outside without a disguise in years. A sense of detachment from regular existence instilled by a life in the limelight, starting when she was all of nineteen.

Each step Heather took brought a new sense of relief as another weight was lifted and the bells of freedom rang. Bonging along with the clock tower as it came to be noon. It was a bit late in the day for the coffee shop, which was one of the first places to open, along with the bakery, but there was still a little time left on the posted hours. Better late than never, really.

The happy bells jangled overhead as the indoors embraced her, a shift in condition sufficient for Heather to take off her wax jacket. More exposed than she had been in years, she draped the jacket over an arm and marched, bold as brass, to the counter, no one even looking her way. There was something to be said for anonymity.

The holly and the jolly were strewn about the room, holiday cheer shouted through a bullhorn at anyone who entered. Nothing too garish, at least to her mind. Heather's heart was warmed like a yule log.

"What can I get ya?" asked the friendly barista.

"White chocolate macchiato."

"Size?"

"Surprise me."

Taking on the challenge, the barista turned to the machine,

directing it like a maestro in its functions. As the rattle and hum went on, Heather went to find a seat at one of the quaint and tiny tables.

"Heather?" came the call as an earthenware mug, decorated with hand-painted ivy along the rim, appeared on the pick-up shelf.

"Thank you," Heather blurted, claiming the cup.

Sipping from the cutely quaint cup, Heather read from the local island rag. Only one name was under the masthead. In addition to being the island's only reporter, Finty Foss was also the photographer, editor, and did the layouts. It wouldn't be too much of a surprise if she did all the printing as well. Holed up in a shed behind her house, hair done in a tight ponytail and sleeves rolled up to her elbows with ink smeared on her cheeks, she ran the manual printing press bequeathed by her grandfather.

Her chuckle was small but heartfelt, the image tickling Heather in the best possible way, in addition to changing her perception of the local muck-raker. Finty's dogged ambition struck her less as a selfish careerist who would push her own mother down the stairs for fame, or just a juicy story, than an attempt to keep an old family tradition alive, any way she could.

Finishing off the last sips of sweetness from the mug, Heather gathered her jacket ready for a long walk back to the pub. If nothing else it would give her lots of time to think.

"Oh, hello," Finty said, shaking off fresh flakes.

"Finty," Heather said.

"I've been wanting to talk to you."

"I know," Heather said.

"Is now a good time?" Finty asked, hedging her bets.

"Yes, but not here."

"But . . . coffee," Finty said, looking thoroughly forlorn.

"Get it to go, I'll wait," Heather said, sitting back down at the table.

Finty did just that and was back to the table in record time, taking a hit of caffeine in a take-out cup with a sippy lid.

"Nigel should be by now," Heather said, heading for the door.

"Nigel?"

"Partridge, the taxi driver. It's a long way back to the pub."

"Pub?" Finty asked.

"Bailey's Barley Barrel. It is where I am staying and where I will talk, if you are still interested."

"Yes, definitely. It is either Bailey's or The Barley Barrel, by the by. Only tourists use all three."

Nestled in the back seat of Nigel's cab, Heather could tell Finty had questions, and not just about her career or how she ended up holidaying there. Letting it lie until the time was right, they both watched the snowflakes smack against the windows, melting on contact.

Chapter Thirteen: The Truth Will Out

Jiminy rolled on her back doing her best to savage the bit of yarn Lily was dangling, both enjoying themselves immensely. The kitty could have been a good visual aid for the interview, but it was best to leave them be.

"Hi, Finty," Lily said, not looking up from the dangling yarn.

"Lily," Finty said from the stairs on the way up.

Up they went to the tiny room rented by the week, set up as a bed-sit. Finty took the chair at the table as Heather seated herself at the foot of the bed.

"Is it okay if I record?" Finty asked, getting out her phone.

"Of course."

Setting up voice recorder, Finty flipped out her mini Moleskine and read through her notes.

"You have notes?" Heather asked.

"Always."

"Can I ask you a question?"

"Sure," Finty said.

"Why do you have a smartphone on an island with no Wi-Fi?"

"There's lots of other uses," Finty replied. "Besides, there is a really good price on the data-plan."

Heather could have smacked herself for not thinking of that. No Wi-Fi didn't mean no internet. There were probably clever sorts on the island who had figured out the miracle of digital calling too. No cellphone reception required. Probably something to do with satellites. Settling into her piece of humble pie, Heather awaited Finty's first question.

"When did you know that you loved music?"

The story flowed like a stream babbling past a cozy charismatic country cottage. She told of her dad's carefully curated collection of vinyls, played on the old-school wood panel record player in the living room, dancing around the couch at eight-years-old., but not really understanding the lyrics, even as the rhythm struck a chord in her soul.

Finty listened intently, making notes in her Moleskine even as the phone recorded. Probably adding supplementary notes for the later article. Heather had certainly seen it before, with some mixed results.

Pushing any potential hatchet jobs out of her mind, giving Finty the benefit of the doubt, Heather answered all the questions that came. Most of them were refreshingly open ended, either to give her space to meander, getting to the heart of the matter, or to dig herself a deeper hole.

She had been wrong before, like when she'd signed with the first label that offered, but she didn't get that sense from Finty. One advantage to getting bitten was you started to recognize the sharks a lot quicker. Finty was ambitious and keen but showed no sign of the near-evil Heather had so recently seen.

"Eggnog?" Lily asked, as Heather and Finty thumped back down the stairs.

"I'm not sure, Silas would know," Heather said.

"No, I mean would you like some?"

"Uh, sure, thanks," Finty said.

Really? Heather mouthed.

"Just go with it, trust me, it's easier," Finty said.

Like a shot, Jiminy was returned to Heather's capable hands, looking only a little confused, as the younger Bailey sibling barreled through the kitchen doors, leaving them banging in her wake.

Getting the kitty napping in her basket upstairs—not difficult after the fun she'd had with Lily—Heather went back downstairs, just in time to hear much clattering, grinding, and a smattering of creative cursing.

Eventually Lily reemerged looking a little worse for wear, with a silver tray carrying three lovely mugs filled to the top, a sprinkling of nutmeg on each light-yellow surface.

Seated properly at a pub table, the three took the first heavenly sip. It wasn't quite the same as what Heather's mom made but was more than enough. Even with everything else going on, there could still be some holiday cheer.

The thump came early, sending Jiminy mewing and purring towards the door, before Heather even had an eye open.

"This early?" Heather asked Jiminy.

Heather hadn't thought of it, but semi-regular newspaper delivery was meant to be a perk of the booking at Bailey's Barley Barrel.

"Let's see what Finty has for us today," Heather said, unfolding the paper as she sat in the only chair.

Jiminy jumped up onto the table to read over her shoulder, like kitty's loved to do, especially when they wanted attention.

"Oh," Heather said, noticing the piece Finty interviewed her for on page three.

Heather tried to keep her nerve, taking it one sentence at a time, letting the piece reveal itself slowly.

It wasn't the worst thing ever penned about her. There had been some real hatchet jobs, especially as she found fame. *2 of Hearts* was generally met with resounding indifference on the part of critics, despite being her feeling it had been best, despite the silly title, but the listeners loved it.

The exposure Heather most feared since taking the ferry over from the city had come, and everything was fine. The sky certainly hadn't fallen.

"Not so bad," Heather said, scratching a concerned looking Jiminy behind the ear.

Heather left the paper on the table and went out to face the day. Considering the paper's circulation topped out at about five hundred, floods of admirers coming in just to see her, let alone getting tracked down, weren't that likely.

"Can you watch Jiminy?" Heather asked Lily, who was setting up at the pub for the day.

"Yippy!" Lily cheered before catching herself. "I mean . . . yes, of course."

"Thanks," Heather said, handing over the basket.

Her kitty secured, Heather went out to meet the taxi which was already running outside.

"So, I hear you're a musician," Nigel said, as Heather got in the back.

"Word spreads fast, hey?"

"Like wildfire," Nigel confirmed.

"Yes, I am a musician," Heather said, with a note of pride.

"Oh, aye, do you enjoy it?"

Heather looked out at the whiteout landscape, searching for an honest answer, not sure herself anymore.

"I did," she said. "And I'm starting to again."

CHAPTER FOURTEEN: A FLY IN THE EGG-NOG

The season was upon them, and there were carols to be sung. Townsfolk started going door to door like yesteryear, except for the Land Rovers used to get between the farther flung farms. The drivers, all volunteers, sipped hot apple cider from thermoses between visits. With not a scrooge to be found on the entire island, the holly sort of jolly did abound during the final countdown.

The spirit seized Jiminy as much as any other, the kitty behaving better than Heather had ever seen. A welcome change from their usual scene, it let Heather work as much as she dared.

Old habits dying hard, she was the type to write on every shard when the muse took hold. No torches or clubs for her, despite what Hemingway might have to say on the matter.

Free of her computer — or any other tech — taking the no Wi-Fi thing literally, she scribbled away on a notebook miraculously found at the corner shop, and a pen borrowed from Lily, usually used to jot down orders.

The words came out as naturally as water flowing downriver. Whatever block she might have had while trapped in the glitz machine fell away, obliterating the Pop Tart she had somehow become, leaving only the singer-songwriter she wanted to be. She didn't even miss her mansion anymore.

As she was syllables away from the final song for her potential new album, the chords written neatly along the top of the lyric lines, there came a tapping at her door, too gentle to even be considered a knock.

"Coming, Lily," Heater called, as Jiminy remained snoozing in her basket.

"How did you know?" Lily asked.

"Just a hunch."

"Betty Highsmith wants to see you. She was about to come up herself, but we don't really allow that. Other than Silas and me, it is paying tenants only."

"Good rule."

"Thanks. Do you want to come down, or should I tell her to go away?"

"If you tell her to go away, will she only come back?"

"Oh, probably."

"Best to just get it over with then."

"If you can," Lily suggested.

"Want to watch Jiminy?"

"Yes, please!"

Lily rushed into the room at a controlled stroll before sitting in the chair at the table and peering into the basket as if waiting for a kettle to boil.

Stifling a chuckle, Heather went down to face the music, expecting it to be a far cry from the carol singing.

Silas was probably off painting somewhere, and there wasn't much in the way of customers during the day. In the otherwise empty pub sat Betty Highsmith at one of the polished tables.

Folding her hands on the table, she looked like a teacher getting ready to chew out a naughty student, despite being not much older than Heather herself.

"Take a seat," Betty commanded.

Heather ignored the meaning behind the clumsy attempt at a power-move and sat down. After a decade of managers, agents, public relations gurus and record executives, Betty

Highsmith held no terror for Heather Fideler.

"Betty," Heather said, keeping cool.

Heather's usual approach was just to smile and nod, only speaking up when absolutely necessary.

"I hear you're famous," Betty said.

"Everything is relative. No one knew who I was around here until last week."

"True, can't say I really did. Your name came up occasionally on my feed, but I always ignored it. I don't have time for all that celebrity news crap. The break-ups and make ups, marriages and divorces, all going around like clockwork."

There had only been one marriage, and one divorce in Heather's case, with little in terms of the usual faff. Her publicists weren't thrilled, but she always did her best to keep her private life private. The paparazzi wouldn't always have it, making up stories when they couldn't find a real one, but none of it did much damage. Then it had happened, the worst ever trick without a whiff of a treat, yanking the rug out from under Heather's feet. The actual proceedings were completed within months. Heather didn't even get a lawyer. They'd never really had a fight, and she had no intention of starting. In the end they worked it out between themselves, the lawyers only involved to make things official. Heather hadn't really felt anything then except for bad. Bad to be losing Jake, and bad it hadn't worked out, when they were both so sure it would. The jarring distinction between her real self and the star persona got to be too much for him to take. The truth of their marriage, and its end, was more a disappointment than a failure. It was also a surprise, because they'd never have had a fight.

"There was only one."

"One what?" Betty asked, stopping mid-sermon.

"One marriage, one divorce. No one even knew we were dating. I never flaunted it. Ever. The paps and tabloids did what they do, but it meant nothing."

"Be that as it may, you are still on the rebound, and Silas has his own things going on."

"You mean Lily?"

"Partly. The bottom line is the last thing he needs is a broken heart. I understand why you would want to be here for Christmas, but after that I seriously suggest you go back to the city and get on with your glamorous life."

"Or what?" Heather asked, surprising even herself.

"What?" Betty asked, stopping mid-stand.

"You were making a threat, right? I need to go back to the city or what?"

"It wasn't a threat," Betty gasped, looking a little shocked.

"Really? Because it certainly wasn't a promise, more of a statement. It falls short of even an ultimatum, because there is no other option. You really aren't good at this whole intimidation thing, are you?"

"Who said I was trying to intimidate you?" Betty asked.

"Other than your body language? Seriously, Betty, if looks could kill I would already be in the morgue. Luckily, I'm used to it. Sit through a *creative meeting* at a corporate record label owned by a parent company that also sells cigarettes and ketchup and then talk to me."

Letting out a little huff, Betty walked away, pride a little bruised but in no way beaten. She would be back.

CHAPTER FIFTEEN: STARTING TO LOOK A LOT LIKE A CHRISTMAS CRISIS

Morning arrived as so many had before — with a kitten attack. Jiminy could be surprisingly nimble when she wanted to be and landed smack on the back of Heather's slumbering head.

"Really?" she asked, opening one eye.

Jiminy licked Heather's ear in reply, the rough kitty tongue driving the idea of sleep from her mind.

"All right, all right." Heather sighed, as Jiminy jumped down from the bed and bounded around the room with sheer elation.

Walked and then fed, Jiminy was less like her name and allowed herself to be put into the basket.

Barely making a sound, the pair went down to the Barley Barrel proper, *Bailey's* not quite fitting right in her mind, probably because of the drink.

"Good morning," Lily quite literally sang.

"Thanks," Heather wheezed, as the younger Bailey took her in a surprisingly crushing attack-hug.

"Breakfast is ready, you can leave the kitty in her basket."

"Is that allowed?" Heather asked.

"I won't tell if you don't," Lily said, with a cheeky wink.

These were deeply practical country types. There was a tradition on Heather's Haven, being so far removed from anywhere else, to do what made most sense at the time, regardless of the assumed rules. Things worked a lot better that way.

Heather found a table near the twinkling tree, nearly sparkling with tinsel and the like, and made plans on what to do with the rest of the day.

Lily managed to do it again; all the foods Heather liked best were laid out before her. Just as she had tucked in, the first of the antique tree decorations tinkled to the hardwood floor.

"Jiminy, no!" Heather yelped, leaping up from her seat as the kitten scaled the trunk of the very real tree at what appeared to be warp speed, leaving the basket behind.

"It's fine," Lily said, coming back in from the kitchen. "Kitties will be kitties."

Taking some time, they found Jiminy deep in the tree near the top. If there was one thing the tiny kitty could do it was climb, a talent honed nearly as sharply as her knack for making trouble. The two, more often than not, worked together.

"There you are," Lily said, gently taking the slightly startled kitten from between the twinkling branches.

"You are going back in my room," Heather scolded.

"I can watch her," Lily offered.

"Are you sure?"

"Positive!"

She certainly was, more than anyone Heather had ever known. It could have just been the Bailey disposition, but growing up on Heather's Haven probably had something to do with it too.

Putting little Jiminy back in her basket carrier, Lily sat at a table nearby and did crosswords while Heather finished eating, the tree none the worse for wear. Even the fallen ornament was replaced without so much as a crack. Another island Christmas miracle, leading Heather to ponder if she wanted to go back to the life she'd had before.

"Who can that be this early?" Lily went to see what she could.

"We want to talk to Heather," said the mayor at the head

of the gathered mob.

"I always have time for a posse," Heather said, as the gang came in.

"Is this true?" the mayor asked, laying a copy of the paper with the story about Heather on the table.

Sensing impending doom, Jiminy did her best to protect her mistress, hissing from inside her basket, but it appeared to have little effect.

"It is," Heather said, bracing for what might come next.

"Oh, good!" The mayor said, nearly deflating into the small chair at the other end of the small table.

"It is?" Heather asked, not quite expecting that reaction.

"Oh, heck yeah, pardon my French, we've had a dickens of a time getting things together for the Christmas concert this year. It had just been one fiasco after another. We've all done our best but are still short of a director."

"Gus, the music teacher at the school, got hit with the flu out of the blue and left us in the lurch, bless him," said Reverend Fordwick, leader of the island's tiny church.

"We thought you could do it," soothed Agnes from the store. "You're so clever and very talented at it. Our Mickey found you on the YouTubes."

"It's just YouTube, gran," Mickey Edwards said, his face tuning a gentle shade of red.

"Whatever the fudge, oh, there I go with the *parlante francaise*," Agnes said, turning a rosy shade to closely match her grandson. "The point is you're great. I should have known from what I heard at the open mic. Those were your original songs right?"

"Right," Heather said, blushing brightly, joining the crowd. "Only thing is, I'm not sure I'd know how. To run a Christmas concert, I mean."

"Don't look at me, I voted against," said Betty.

"I wasn't," Heather said bluntly.

"Will you just try and see?" Agnes asked.

"Okay," Heather said, the pleas of the sweet old lady — and the whole town council really, aside from Betty — getting the best of the harder parts of her personality.

"Wonderful," said the mayor with relief. "The next planning meeting is this afternoon."

"So soon?" Heather asked, only half joking.

"Indeed, we need to stay on the ball, we only have a week."

"A week!" Heather squeaked.

CHAPTER SIXTEEN: UNDER THE MISTLE-TOE

Christmas Eve arrived on a holly-scented breeze, whipping the islanders into a frenzy of fun as final preparations were made for the big day.

Directions on Heather's Haven could be vague, an *if you get to the old bridge, you've gone too far* sort of system that was common to rural areas. Most folk knew the lay of the land and tended to think of it in the most abstract and literal terms.

"Hello, hon, no kitty today?" Agnes asked, as Heather jangled through the door.

"Oh, no, Jiminy is with Lily."

"Make sense, Lily loves kitties, animals in general really. She's been horse riding since she was wee. I think she used to say she wanted to be a veterinarian."

It was like something from a story book, or at least a middle-grade novel, but it also explained a heck of a lot.

"Why didn't she?" Heather asked, afraid she already knew the answer.

"Didn't have the grades, in math anyway. She's a clever girl in some ways, as sweet as blueberry pie, but math and science aren't really her forte."

Heather found herself relating to the younger Bailey's situation. Despite her musical background, the math of it was never her thing. Never really able to comprehend written music, she still mostly played and wrote by ear and the chord symbols which were more alphabetical than anything. Then again, Paul McCartney did the same thing, hiring someone to write it out when traditional notation was needed.

"Do you have any maps?"

"Maps?" Agnes asked, like Heather was speaking a foreign language.

"Of the island."

"Oh, yes, I think so."

Following some rummaging under the desk, Agnes blew the dust from an ancient map that looked like it was printed around the same time as the Gutenberg Bible.

"Should be mostly the same," Agnes said, spreading out the map on the counter.

"Right," Heather said. The official diagram of the island looking like a map of Middle Earth.

"Is that . . . Latin?"

"Oh, probably, we've been here for a while."

Try as she might, Heather just couldn't make head or tail of the thing, actually turning it around a few times, just to be sure.

"A bit odd, isn't it?" Agnes asked.

"Yeah," Heather confessed.

"Where are you trying to get, dear?"

"The town hall. I need to help with the setup for the Christmas concert tomorrow."

"Ah yes, all the meetings have finally become manifest."

"Exactly, words are one thing, actual construction is another," Heather agreed.

"Why don't you drive down with Silas?"

"He's painting," Heather said, a little heat touching her cheeks at the very mention of his name.

"Nigel?"

"I didn't want to bother him. Not when I was told I could walk."

"Probably not," Agnes said bluntly. "You're probably best

calling Nigel. The Haven isn't very big, but you still don't want to get lost."

"Do you have a phone I can use? My plan expired and I can't get online to renew it."

"Of course."

"Oh, aye, no problem, love," Nigel said on the other end. "Sonny Jim'll be there in two shakes."

"Sonny Jim?" Heather asked, after hanging up.

"The son in Partridge & Son," Agnes explained.

"Oh, right."

Within five minutes, Jim Partridge eased the second cab up to the curb outside the corner shop with skill and aplomb. Agnes tucked the map back under the counter, in case it was ever needed again.

Jim was the spitting image of his father, right down to the coat and cap. The only major difference was he was about thirty years young, making up for the gap in relative experience with sheer enthusiasm.

"Where to?" he asked.

"The town hall."

Much to her shock, the young cabbie took the most direct route between points A and B, with no real tricks or meandering to try and drive up the fare. Within fifteen minutes they were there. Jim dropped her off at the door of the hall after a route Heather barely followed at all. Even if she'd managed to find her way there on foot, she surely would have been quite late. With Jim's assistance, she was right on time.

"Thanks again," she said, paying the reasonable fare.

"Anytime."

Jim's cab disappeared into the woods that separated the hall from the rest of the island, leaving Heather to quietly wonder if he had ever really been there at all.

The hall was buzzing when Heather arrived. The islanders of Heather's haven were keeners of the first order, something

Heather Fideler would do well to remember if she decided to stay, a notion that appealed to her more all the time.

"You made it," Silas said, making Heather's heart go thud.

"Yes, I–I did. What are you doing here?"

It came out more as an accusation than she meant but Heather was just so flustered she couldn't help it.

"Just lending a hand. Betty said they needed more big strong men for the heavy lifting, I think in the literal sense, and I won't be doing anything until later tonight."

"She actually said *big, strong men*?"

"Not in so many words, but the implication was clear, though I don't think she called anyone else. I just put it down as a ploy to get me to help."

"Makes sense," Heather said, staring daggers right at Betty's back as she helped with the gingerbread house competition.

"Most think it's cute. At least that is what we tell ourselves. It is just her way in any case, and we just have to live with it."

"Pretty accepting place, isn't it?" Heather asked, thinking out loud.

"We kind of have to be," Silas said sagely.

"How so?"

"The island is a little small to have enemies. I mean where are you going to go, other than back to the city? A little bit of teeth-gritting civility is a small price to pay, I'd say, speaking only for myself."

The tall handsome man had a point. He was basically ten years her senior, so it shouldn't have come as too much of a surprise. It was also a comfort to know he could see it from both sides. Twenty-one years in the city, by her estimations, before a further sixteen or so on Heather's Haven.

Both the city and the island had a lot to offer in different ways and different people, but the older she got the more Heather could see the charms of a simpler life. She'd been famous and glamorous, living her best version of the big city life. Maybe it was time she tried to be herself again, with no distinction between her private and public existence.

"Hey, look, mistletoe," Silas said, noticing the sprig of greenery hung above them.

"Well, would you look at that."

"Do you hold to traditions?" Silas asked, turning very serious.

"You bet I do," Heather enthused.

Standing on her tiptoes in an attempt to match his commanding height, Heather put everything she had into that one sweet kiss, making it just right.

CHAPTER SEVENTEEN: CHRISTMAS CONCERT CATASTROPHE!

The weather blew outside the old pub, making the shingle quietly swing in the breeze. December made itself known as it hadn't for years. Some of the vehicles stopped because of frozen gears.

"Do you have everything?" Lily asked, entertaining Jiminy with a bit of string.

Heather did a double-check just to be sure. It had been her suggestion that Lily ask on the way out. The Christmas concert was like Woodstock and the Super Bowl rolled into one. Everyone would be there from every corner of the island, which was why they had to use the hall. It was the only building Heather's Haven had where everyone could fit, at least at a distance that would also allow them to turn all the way around without bumping anything.

"Got it," Heather said, going through the list for the tenth time.

It was far from her first rodeo. True, there were usually stagehands and grips and the like to do the really dirty work during her concerts, but she'd seen it all going on, and was in no way surprised by the work involved putting on even a tiny community show.

"Got everything?" Silas asked, as they lifted Heather's load into the truck.

"Yes, Lily already asked."

"Good."

Giving Heather a kiss as he closed the back of the pick-up, Silas hopped in and started up, back into business mode. There would be no one at the pub that night, not with the concert at the same time. A few might drift in afterwards, but that was about it.

Heather studied Silas as they drove, the old and dirty snow crunching beneath the new snow tires on the old truck.

She was searching for a sign, a scar or something that might show what Betty had mentioned. If he was in pain, from heartbreak or otherwise, Silas hid it well. Probably to stay brave for Lily and she could see how.

Silas would probably act like everything was fine even if his soul was burning in Hell. That was big brothers for you, especially when they had a gap like that. Far as Heather could tell, Silas was more like Lily's dad.

"Do I have something on my face?" Silas asked.

"What?" Heather asked, startled back to reality.

"You were staring, I thought maybe something was wrong."

"Is there?" Heather asked, before she could stop herself.

"What do you mean?"

Heather wracked her brain for a way to proceed that wouldn't make her look like a total git.

"I heard you were ... wounded ... by *love.*"

"My goodness, you *are* a songwriter aren't you," Silas chuckled.

"Yeah, I guess," Heather said, trying to hold onto a shred of her dignity.

Whatever Betty was about would have to wait. Right then Heather just wanted to enjoy the day and the coming night. She had made her feelings pretty clear, and Silas, bless him, was responding in kind. The future beyond Christmas wasn't quite certain but there was something between them to keep in mind as she planned the next steps in her life.

"Ready?" Silas asked, as they pulled up to the hall for the final preparations.

"Let's do this."

Crunching in the snow like they'd planned it, Silas helped shlep the last of the needed supplies and equipment into the hall. Everything was nearly ready and was perfect to Heather's star-struck eyes.

"You look like you might cry," Silas said.

"I might," Heather agreed.

Sweetly and discreetly, Silas passed her his hanky, cream white Irish linen with his initials, SB, monogrammed into the lower left edge.

"Thank you," Heather said, before wiping her eyes and blowing her nose with a honk that could attract geese.

It had been a lot of work, but she'd found something like peace for the first time in as long as she could remember.

It was only a few hours until the doors would open and the first few guests would be trickling in. Everyone not on the town council or recruited like Heather had been kept well away until all was ready. Nothing was going to get her down. Not even the dirty looks Betty kept casting her way, especially when Heather and Silas got close, which they did a lot. There hadn't exactly been an announcement, but the knowledge Heather and Silas liked each other was getting to be as common as a loaf of bread.

Most accepted it and were even happy. Then there were those like Betty, who seemed to resent Heather even more, if such a thing were possible. Heather had encountered envy before, the green-eyed monster no stranger in the business of show. Only their rivals and enemies were less likely to make it known. It could have simply been her former life that caused Betty to despise her, but it was starting to feel almost like a personal vendetta, like anyone who got close to Silas would feel Betty Highsmith's wrath.

"Hey, are you okay?" Silas asked.

"Uh, yeah, fine."

"Your knuckles are white."

"Oh, right," Heather said, glancing down at her clenched fists. "It's a, uh, relaxation exercise."

She made a show of clenching her fists and letting go until Silas seemed satisfied with her little white lie. It stung to be dishonest, but she didn't want to bring him down with the truth. Vowing to have the most wonderful evening ever, even if it killed her, Heather focused her mind on the event before her, not whatever might have happened in the past.

The doors opened at the appointed time, the schedule running along smoothly, or at least as written. Nearly every one of the chairs set up in the hall was taken when it was time to begin. The few spots left here and there, mostly at the edges, were for the performers when they finished their sets.

It wasn't all Christmas music, despite the name, though most did a rendition of a better-known holiday tune. Mike Greer's rendition of *Here We Come A-Wassailing* on the hurdy gurdy a particular, and peculiar, stand out.

The end of the evening grew near, and the mood became clear. Almost everyone wanted Heather to step out of her organizer role and play.

"What do you say?" Agnes asked.

"I didn't bring my guitar," Heather said, which was true enough.

"Oh, I'm sure Nigel won't mind."

"Are you sure?"

"I'll go ask," Agnes said, before Heather could object.

A few moments later, Agnes came back holding the guitar in both hands, as if it was Excalibur.

Nigel's guitar was a Taylor, one of the best, and most expensive, kind around. It was also vintage, pure wood instruments following an opposite logic to most things, actually getting better with age.

Getting the high-grain leather strap over her head and into position, Heather stepped out onto the stage and up to the mic. She'd rarely been so nervous in all her life. Stages and shows were a dawdle most of the time, but not in such an intimate space, in front of so many people she liked. Even Finty Foss had become something like a friend, after the dread of exposure had finally passed. For the first time in a long time, there was something to prove, and she didn't want to screw it up. Fingers shaking only a little, she started to pluck the perfectly set and tuned strings, every note seeming to ring through the massive hall. Checking that she remembered all the lyrics, and in order, Heather Fideler, erstwhile Pop Star, finally returned to her roots, leaned into the mic, and sang. Like a leak in a dam, once it started, it wouldn't stop. An old switch flipped and the songs just kept on comping. She sang nothing written for her by the label, but rather holiday standards, giving them her own particular flavour, like her mom's homemade eggnog. Last up that night, she had all the time she could want, there were no other hopefuls waiting in the wings. When her catalog of Holiday cheer was at an end, her own songs kicked in. The ones from her first two albums, when she was still allowed to write, and the one she'd finished just that week, still sitting between the covers of that notebook in her room at the pub, waiting to see what might happen.

Finally, she hit the last song. The album ender and the showstopper. The polite applause, encouraging whoops and frequent sing-alongs that had accompanied the previous songs were struck silent by the moment. The song called *O Silas* emerged from her voice and guitar by way of her heart.

Silence reigned, the final note ringing and refusing to fade. No one dared to even cough or ruin the perfect moment until the door to the hall opened and Silas left with Betty

Highsmith.

CHAPTER EIGHTEEN: FAST EXIT

The applause faded to a hum as Heather tried to focus, waiting to wake up from what had to be the worst sort of dream. A notion she'd convinced herself of, despite the weight of the guitar on her shoulder and slight bite of leather on the exposed part of her neck.

Silas was gone, and so was his truck, or so she assumed. It only stood to reason. He'd probably known Betty for years, sixteen of them at least. Heather was just a Janey Come Lately, hoping she might belong. That didn't explain the kisses, let alone the handkerchief, still in the pocket of her jeans, but maybe that was just how people showed affection around there. Goodness knew they were weird enough.

The applause turned into a standing ovation and Heather took a bow. Entirely on autopilot, she left the stage, passing the guitar back to Agnes as she left.

Heather didn't cry, not all at once. It took time to get the confusion and seething anger before the true and twisting agony could come through. Two men in less than a year, what the heck was wrong with her? To his credit, Jake had never cheated, but that wasn't really the solace she hoped it would be.

Silas hadn't really either. There were indications galore, but they ever actually made it official, as the saying went. There was certainly an understanding, at least on her end, but how far did that really go?

An old, cold pain stabbed her in the chest, despite the relatively mild evening, never mind the warmth of the wax jacket.

It didn't even occur to try and get a ride, even with Nigel or Jim. She just had to get away from everyone and get back to her life. The dream was nice, but it was time to wake up. There were no Christmas miracles, at least not for the likes of her.

Out of the hall in a hurry, trying to avoid any well-meaning townsfolk, Heather made for a change of scenery. Soon trudging through the old and dirty snow, crushed low on what would otherwise be the road, new flakes started to fall, only adding to the banks on either side, already too tall for her to get off the road. Luckily, everyone was still at the concert and would be for a while, giving a decent window before there would be any vehicles coming up behind her. An advantage to the snow, despite the increasing cold, was that it helped to make things a lot brighter, reflecting the moonlight, cast down from the clear winter sky, letting her see where she was going, even if she only had the foggiest idea of where she was heading.

After two hours and a few wrong turns, the old bridge having been a particular challenge, Heather could again see the seasonal light strung all around downtown.

Heather's calves complaining, her eyes nearly frozen shut, but she knew where she was going and was almost where she needed to be.

To keep her mind busy while she trekked, Heather ran through the steps over and over in her head. She would pack as quickly as possible while Jiminy watched, then she would call Nigel and get the ferry back to the city that very night. Everything that had happened with Silas and the island already seemed like a dream.

"Hello," Lily said, sitting on the floor of the pub, playing with Jiminy.

"Aren't you at the Christmas concert?" Heather asked with a start.

"No, silly, I'm here. Someone had to watch the kitty. She could get into all sorts of mischief otherwise."

Simple as it was, she couldn't argue with Lily's logic. She didn't mean to be, but Jiminy could be a real handful sometimes.

Just about to whisk the kitty away from her new best friend, it registered with Heather just how much fun Jiminy and Lily were having together. It really wouldn't be fair to punish Lily for what her brother did or didn't do. Leaving the two to their play, Heather made her way upstairs to try and defrost before packing.

Peeling out of her jeans, which were basically frozen to her legs, Heather sat in front of the heater in her underwear for nearly an hour until the feeling returned to her extremities.

"Right," she said, when freedom of movement returned.

As the rolls filled the space inside the suitcase, questions rose like whack-a-mole in her mind. Another popped up as she knocked one down with the hammer of anger and logic.

With her bags packed and set beside the room door, dressed in a fresh tracksuit, Heather went down to the pub proper to call a cab.

"Can I use the phone?" she asked Lily.

"Of course, as long as it's a local call."

"You're kidding, right?" Heather bit back after a short pause.

"Yeah, I am."

Behind the bar, Heather dialed Nigel as something like logic returned to her mind. She couldn't quite remember the number, but it was printed on the card behind the bar next to the phone. She pressed the buttons on the touchtone, each strike on the keypad making its own sort of sound. The rings went through with a little buzz of static at the end of each, indicating a pretty bad connection. No doubt on account of the weather.

"Hello, Partridge & Son," Nigel said, sounding a little winded.

"I need a cab."

"Well, you've called the right place. At least it would be if not for the weather. We won't be taking any more fares tonight, it's not safe."

"Because of the storm?" Heather asked.

"Because of the storm," Nigel confirmed.

"No ferries then?"

"Not until the morning. It's safest just to stay inside."

"What will happen if I don't?"

"Hard to say," Nigel said. "You'd probably freeze to death if you went to wait for the ferry."

"Right," Heather said, considering her options, the whole freezing to death thing not sounding so bad.

"Stay inside," Nigel said.

It came out as an order, as if he'd heard the hesitation in her voice and knew she was considering it.

"Okay," Heather said. A little defeated, she hung up the phone.

"You leavin'?" Lily appeared by her side like an apparition, cuddling Jiminy.

"Gah! Don't sneak up on me like that, I'm old and might have a heart attack."

"I thought you were twenty-eight," Lily said.

"Oh yeah," Heather said, as if she'd just remembered.

"You're silly," said sweet little Lily with a giggle to melt Heather's heart.

Dying in a storm didn't seem as appealing as before, even if she couldn't get away until the next day. What happened at the Christmas concert still stung like a swarm of specially mutated nuclear hornets, but Heather could get over it, probably. She was still a little bruised and scarred, at least on the inside, from October, but she had gotten through that okay, for the most part. She was still breathing at the very least and planned to be for a long time. There was still a lot to hang around for.

"What happened?" Lily asked.

"What do you mean?"

"You look a little . . . ookie."

"Mysterious and spooky?" Heather asked.

"No . . . just a little ookie," Lily said, thinking it over.

Even Jiminy leaned in for a closer look just to be sure. Her little kitty nose twitched as she checked that Heather smelled right.

"Good to know," Heather said, scratching Jiminy behind the ear.

"Eggnog?"

"Sure, why not? I'd like to drink it up in my room though."

"Suit yourself."

CHAPTER NINETEEN: THE MORNING AFTER

The Dickensian myth didn't hold true. There were no ghostly visitors in the night, bringing light to a heart and soul riddled with anger and blight. Not even a cricket to be found in the accursed morning light. Just a kitty, of a similar name, Jiminy without the cricket.

Curled up at the foot of the small bed where Heather had been sleeping for nearly a month, the little kitty purred in her sleep. A bit more out of the ordinary was the adorable little cuddle bug lying next to her, still fast asleep.

Heather cleared back some hair that had fallen into Lily's face, tucking it behind her ear. They'd only really known each other a few weeks, but she was already feeling like the little sister Heather never had. They could have been sisters-in-law if things had worked out with Silas.

Flinching a bit, Heather forced the thought from her mind, focusing on Lily's sweetly slumbering face instead. If there was to be any hope, at least for Heather's faith in humanity, it was there.

"Oof, Jiminy!" Lily cried, as the kitty pounced on her back, the torch truly passed.

"She does that every morning," Heather said.

"You mean it is Christmas?"

"Yeah, I suppose it is," Heather gently teased.

Like a shot, Lily was up and off to where they kept the tree, Jiminy bounding behind her.

Letting out a laugh once they were past earshot, Heather went down to, just to see what all the fuss was about.

"That wasn't there before," Heather said, meaning the pile of perfectly wrapped presents under the tree.

"Of course not, Santa came!" Lily said.

"You believe in Santa?" Heather blurted.

"I believe in presents, and here they are!"

"True enough," Heather said, going over to join in the fun.

There was a tiny gift for Jiminy, with a new leash and harness, as well as a knit ball full of catnip which she started batting around immediately.

"There's a few here for you!" Lily said, passing Heather the pile.

Struck speechless by the fact of it, she started unwrapping, starting at the bottom with something she was almost certain would be a cassette tape, not quite able to believe that such a thing could be true.

"H-how did you get this?" Heather asked, staring at an original green-label edition of her demo tape.

"I don't know what you mean," Lily said innocently. "Santa brought it."

"Santa."

Lily gave a wink, letting Heather in on the little joke. It suddenly became quite clear exactly who was meant by the term.

"Where is Silas, shouldn't he be here?" Heather asked.

"Probably at home. He had a busy night."

"Yeah, I *bet* he did," Heather grumbled.

"He got Betty into a taxi, before the storm, and then helped dismantle everything from the concert after it was over. He must be pooped."

"Taxi?"

"Yeah, he called me after it happened. Said she got a bit excited about something, and he called Nigel to take her home. Said he would see us this morning, which seemed like wishful thinking."

"He put Betty in a taxi then went back into the hall?" Heather asked, realizing the mistake she had made.

"Yeah, he said he hadn't noticed you leave but looked for you there after she was gone, but you had already left. It was a bit silly walking all the way back from the town hall. Especially with the blizzard. he had to wait for things to clear up before he could come back."

"Do you know where he is now?" Heather asked, suddenly intense.

"Probably in bed, if not, then painting."

"Painting?"

"Out on the coast. It is a bit of a tradition. Every Christmas morning, he goes out and paints the scene that year."

Up like a jack-in-the-box, Heather went to the phone, only hoping against hope Nigel or Jim would be driving that day.

"Partridge & Son, the son speaking."

"Jim!"

"Oh, hey Heather."

"I need a cab!"

"Well, yes, I gathered that."

"Now!"

"I'll be right there."

True to his word, it was less than ten minutes before Jim was outside, blowing his horn to get her attention.

"Where are you going?"

"To get your brother, I just hope it isn't too late. Watch Jiminy, okay?"

"Okay!"

Into the cab they roared away, Heather only hoping she could remember exactly which bit of coastline they'd had their picnic. It wasn't a sure thing but was all she had to go on.

"Where are we going exactly?" Jim asked, after the fifth

vague direction.

"Do you know where Silas Bailey likes to paint seascapes?"

"Oh, aye," Jim said, and aimed his cab that way.

After what seemed like an eternity they came to the place, finding Silas, easel, truck and all, painting the perspective of that Christmas day.

"Need me to wait?" Jim asked.

"No, with any luck it will be okay," Heather said, paying the fare.

"Godspeed," Jim said, encouragingly.

Casually as she could, Heather moseyed over to where Silas was dubbing a near perfect rendition of the scene before him onto the canvas.

"I waited for you," Silas said, not turning around.

"Yeah, it looked like you had your hands full."

"I sure did," Silas said with a chuckle. "Our cousin can be pretty rowdy when she's riled. It took me and Nigel to get her into the cab."

"Your *cousin!*" Heather yelped.

"Aye, on our mother's side. Didn't inherit her disposition, I can tell you that much."

"No, I guess not," Heather said, nearly gagging on all the humble pie.

A silence fell over the salt-scented scene as Heather tried to fathom what she could say next.

"I don't want you to leave," Silas said, saving her the trouble.

"You don't?"

"No. You seem so happy here. Lily absolutely adores you, if you hadn't noticed."

"I have, I adore her too. It's weird, after so short a time, but she's like the little sister I never had," Heather gushed.

"Yeah, she can have that effect," Silas said, the ghost of a smile haunting his rugged features.

"I want to stay, I just thought after last night . . . it's complicated, and I made a mistake."

"Figured as much, doesn't matter though."

"It doesn't?" Heather asked, hopeful.

"Heck no, I still love you."

The breath caught in Heather's throat. She'd hoped he might, especially after noticing she felt the same, but actually hearing him say it was an altogether different thing.

"Are you shocked?"

"No!" Heather blurted. "I mean, surprised, yes, but more delighted. Much more, actually."

Setting down his brush, Silas stood to his full commanding height and turned to face her. Carefully, deliberately, he got down on one knee, as though in slow motion, and took her hand.

Heather did her best not to cry as Silas addressed her with his wise brown eyes, which had already seen more than a man twice his age.

"Heather Fideler, sorry I don't know your middle name."

"Bridgid."

"After the goddess?" Silas asked.

"I think so."

"How fitting. Heater Brigid Fideler, will you stay here with me and we will see what we can see?"

"Of course," Heather said, though she'd expected a slightly different question to be popped.

Epilogue: All's Well That Ends Well

Bells rang like at Notre Dame as groups of customers trooped through the Barley Barrel's door and out of the cold while Lily saw to the tables and Silas tended the bar. Jiminy lay snoozing in a basket at the back. Seated on the best stool as Jim ran the mixing-boards, Heather played holiday standards old and new, each with her own little twist.

"Any requests?" Heather asked, finishing off a cover of *Christians and Pagans*.

"*O Silas!*" came a voice from the back that sounded suspiciously like Betty's.

Tweaking the tuning a little, she played the request, her gaze never far from the man behind the bar. Not quite her husband, not until that coming May, but her friend, love and soulmate just the same.

ABOUT THE AUTHOR

Born in Toronto, T.S. McNeil grew up on novels and comedy movies.

Moving to B. C., he earned a degree in Art History in 2009 and has been writing in some way since the age of 8.

Discovering the legit jokes in *Four Weddings and A Funeral*, he took on romantic comedy as his main genre.

He lives in a cabin in the woods with his dog and several squirrels, and firmly believes that The Smiths would have been better as a trio.